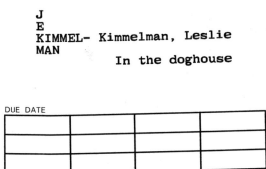

DUE DATE

In the Doghouse

An Emma and Bo Story

by **Leslie Kimmelman**

illustrated by

True Kelley

Holiday House / New York

To Socks,
and to Jodie, Mishka, and Sasha—
the past and present dogs of Plankey's place
L. K.

To Eloise and Charlotte Lindblom
T. K.

Reading level: 2.4

Text copyright © 2006 by Leslie Kimmelman
Illustrations copyright © 2006 by True Kelley
All Rights Reserved
Printed in the United States of America
The illustrations are rendered in pen and ink and watercolor.
www.holidayhouse.com
First Edition
1 3 5 7 9 10 8 6 4 2

Library of Congress Cataloging-in-Publication Data
Kimmelman, Leslie.
In the doghouse : an Emma and Bo story / by Leslie Kimmelman ;
illustrated by True Kelley. — 1st ed.
p. cm.
Summary: When the Lewis family goes on vacation to the lake, Emma gets mad at
her best friend Bo, the family dog, so he runs away to look for a new best friend.
ISBN 0-8234-1882-0 (hardcover)
[1. Dogs—Fiction. 2. Lost and found possessions—Fiction. 3. Vacations—Fiction.]
I. Kelley, True, ill. II. Title.

PZ7.K56493Inat 2006
[E]—dc22
2004047466

ISBN-13: 978-0-8234-1882-4
ISBN-10: 0-8234-1882-0

contents

chapter 1.
On Our Way

Emma and Bo are best friends.
Bo goes wherever Emma goes.
This summer they are going
to the lake.
Emma's mother and father pack
the car.

Mrs. Lewis worries.

"Did you turn off the oven?"

she asks Mr. Lewis.

Mr. Lewis goes into the house.

"I'll help pack," Emma tells her mother.

She puts her toys and books in the car.

Bo helps pack too.

He packs his box of Woofy Treats.

Mrs. Lewis worries some more.
"Did you shut the windows?
Did you turn off the lights?"
she asks Mr. Lewis.
Mr. Lewis goes back
into the house.

Mrs. Lewis climbs behind the wheel.
"Don't forget to lock the front door!"
she calls to Mr. Lewis.
Emma and Bo climb into the backseat.
"Move over, Bo," Emma says.

Emma's mother drives down
the street.
"We are on our way!" she cheers.
"Did we bring toothbrushes?"
"We did," answers Emma.
"Did we bring warm sweaters?"
she asks.
"Yes," answers Emma.
"Did we bring bug spray?
Did we bring tennis rackets?"
she asks.
"We did," answers Emma.
"Are we missing anything at all?"
asks Mrs. Lewis, still worrying.
"Woof!" barks Bo. "Woof, woof!"

"Pipe down, Bo," Emma scolds.

Bo jumps into the front seat.

"Woof, woof!" he barks again.

"Bo!" shouts Emma. "You are right!

We *are* missing something."

Screech! Mrs. Lewis turns
the car around.

Mr. Lewis is sitting on the front steps.

"Yippee!" he shouts.

He climbs into the car.

"The oven is off," says Mr. Lewis.

"The lights are off.

The windows and doors are locked.

And we are on our way."

"We are *all* on our way!"

cheers Emma.

chapter 2.
Emma and Bo Together

Emma and Bo play together
at the lake.
Bo swims whenever Emma swims.
"Careful," calls Mrs. Lewis, worrying.
"Don't get too wet!"

Emma and Bo chase frogs at the lake.

Mr. and Mrs. Lewis play tennis.
Emma and Bo chase their balls.
But Bo just slobbers on them.

Emma and Bo lie in the grass
and look at clouds together.
Emma sees a dragon. It blows away.
Bo sees an enormous bone. "Woof!"
He leaps in the air.
"Down, Bo," Emma tells him.
"You can't catch that bone.
How about a Woofy Treat instead?"

Crrunchh!

Emma and Bo share a hammock
at the lake.

"Move over, Bo," says Emma.

"I'm falling off."

Emma and Bo share a bicycle
at the lake.

Bo! I can't see!

They share Emma's sleeping bag
and the front-porch swing.

But Emma does not want
to share her Popsicle.
Not even with Bo.
"No, Bo, no! It's mine!"
Bo does not listen.
He jumps up and grabs it.

He eats every single lick.

"Bad dog, Bo. Go away!

Go jump in the lake," Emma shouts.

Bo makes sad eyes at Emma.

Emma is mad.

She does not look at him.
Bo licks the special spot
behind her knees.
Emma is still mad. Very mad.
"You are in the doghouse now,"
she yells. "Now get lost! Scram!"

chapter 3.
Bo Alone

Bo is running away.

Emma doesn't like him.

He needs a new home.

He needs a new best friend.

Maybe he'll find one

on the other side of the lake.

Bo meets a small white dog.

Sniff.

Wag.

Drool.

Yip.

The dogs are friends.

They travel around the lake together.
At a white house they smell apple pie
cooling on the windowsill.
"Shoo! Shoo!" shouts the
woman in the red hat.

They see a rabbit in a grassy field.
The dogs are fast,
but the rabbit is faster.
Bo wags his tail.
This is fun!

They see a farmhouse.
"ROOF!" A big brown dog with
big yellow teeth chases them away.
But Bo isn't worried.
He is with his friend.

The small white dog keeps running.
Hey, wait! Oh no!
Bo's friend has
run away.

Bo is all alone again.

The sun is hot,

but the lake is cool.

Glub, glub.

Bo tries to make friends with the fish,

but they swim away.

"Bad dog!" the fishermen shout.

Buzz, buzz.

Bo tries to make friends with a bee,

but it stings him on the nose.

Bo is hungry.

He is tired.

His nose hurts.

His paws hurt.

He wants to go home.

But Bo is lost.

He waits by the side of the road.

chapter 4.
Friends Again

Emma's friend Sam is visiting.
Emma and Sam swim in the lake.
Sam splashes, just like Bo.

Emma and Sam fly kites.

"Careful!" calls Mrs. Lewis, worrying.

"Keep your feet on the ground!"

Emma and Sam make funny faces
and imagine flying high up in the sky.

Emma and Sam look at clouds.

"Mine's a firefighter," says Sam.

"Mine's a big sad dog," says Emma.

Emma's and Sam's parents play tennis.

Emma and Sam chase the balls.

No one slobbers on them.

Emma and Sam each get a snack.

Then Sam goes home.

Now Emma reads in the hammock.

Wait—something is not right.

There is too much room.

"Dad! Mom!" she calls. "Where is Bo?"

Mr. Lewis hasn't seen Bo.

Mrs. Lewis is worried.

This time, Emma is worried too.

When she told Bo to get lost,

she didn't really mean it.

Mrs. Lewis gets in the car.
"Maybe Bo went down the road,"
she says.

Mr. Lewis goes in the house
to get some Woofy Treats.

Emma climbs in the backseat.
"Don't forget Dad," she reminds
her mom.

The Lewises drive past
a little white dog.

They drive past a woman
wearing a red hat and eating pie.
They pass a
fierce-looking
farm dog.

They ask some grumpy fishermen,
"Have you seen our dog?"
"He scared away our fish," one says.
He points to a bump at the side
of the road.

"Bo?" whispers Emma.

"Wo-wo-wooof!" barks Bo.

Slurp! Bo slobbers on Emma's face.

"How about a visit to the
  ice-cream shop?" asks Mrs. Lewis.
"Yippee!" says Mr. Lewis.
  Emma buys her favorite flavor,
  but Bo doesn't even look at it.
  He eats a Woofy Treat instead.
"I missed you, Bo," says Emma.
  Bo wags his tail. *Thump, thump.*

"Whoops!" cries Emma.
By-mistake-on-purpose,
she drops a whole scoop
of ice cream on the floor.
Bo slurps up the mess quickly,
so Emma won't get in trouble.
After all, what are best friends for?

SWCC 6/15